5 reasons why we think you'll love this book

Join Maya as she flies through the air to save the day

Meet the beautiful birds of the kingdom and their fairy friends

Prepare for an epic journey to bring winter to the kingdom

The natural world is full of wonder—turn to the back for fascinating facts!

Colouring in has never been so magical!

To the keeper of this book—it's time
for you to visit the magical kingdom
waiting within. Believe in yourself—that
will give you wings to fly!

To Mia and Molly Duncan.

Illustrated by Dave Shephard, based on
original artwork by Rosie Butcher.

OXFORD
UNIVERSITY PRESS

Great Clarendon Street, Oxford OX2 6DP
Oxford University Press is a department of the University of Oxford.
It furthers the University's objective of excellence in research, scholarship,
and education by publishing worldwide. Oxford is a registered trade mark of
Oxford University Press in the UK and in certain other countries

Text copyright © Anne Booth 2019
Illustrations copyright © Rosie Butcher 2019
The moral rights of the author have been asserted
Database right Oxford University Press (maker)

First published 2019

British Library Cataloguing in Publication Data

Data available

ISBN: 978-0-19-276629-8

1 3 5 7 9 10 8 6 4 2

Printed in India
Paper used in the production of this book is a natural,
recyclable product made from wood grown in sustainable forests.

Magical Kingdom of Birds

of Birds

The Snow Goose

ANNE BOOTH

Illustrated by Rosie Butcher

OXFORD
UNIVERSITY PRESS

Chapter One

Maya was so happy! Her big sister Lauren had already been home from university for a week and they were having lots of fun together. They had been to the pantomime, and she and Lauren had bought presents at the Christmas market, and watched some lovely Christmassy films. To make things even better, it had been snowing in the night, and today, for the first time, the garden was full of bright, cold whiteness, the bare trees standing out like spiky black ink drawings against a pale blue sky. Little dark silhouettes of birds huddled up together in the trees.

'Come on Maya, let's build a snowman!' said Lauren at breakfast, looking out at the white-blanketed garden. 'Dad and Penny will get a nice surprise when they come back from shopping, and my friends Pete and Emily are coming to visit today—let's show them what we can do!'

'I didn't know Pete and Emily were coming,' said Maya. Lauren had told her lots about her friends Pete and Emily and shared pictures of them. They looked as though they had so much fun together at university. Lauren had told Maya what kind friends they were and how they all helped each other out. Maya had wanted to meet them for ages, but now they were actually coming, she felt a bit shy.

'Right, we'll need a carrot for a nose, something for the eyes and mouth, and a hat,' said Lauren. 'We've got to do something to make it extra special though, as Pete's already shared a picture of an enormous snowman he made, so it's going to be tricky to impress him.'

'First of all I need to clear the ice from the birdbath, clear the bird table of snow, and make sure the birds have enough to eat,' said Maya. 'It's hard for them in the snow.'

'I'll help,' said Lauren. Maya pushed the snow off the bird table, put some more bird food out, and hung up a new seed ball. Lauren poured hot water on the iced-up birdbath and made sure there was fresh water for the birds to drink. A little robin, watching from a tree, dashed down and had a sip as soon as she had finished. It was quickly joined by a sparrow and a blackbird.

'That was a good idea, Maya, to check that the birds were OK first,' said Lauren. 'Now, what can we do to make our snowman better than Pete's?' Lauren frowned in concentration as she gazed at the snow.

'Wait a minute,' said Maya. 'Why don't we do something completely different? Why not make a snow bird, not a snowman?'

'Hey, that's not a bad idea,' laughed Lauren. 'What bird, though? You're the expert!'

Maya thought. She knew so much

about birds—she had pictures of them all over her room and she loved watching films and reading books about them. Best of all, she liked to watch them herself, either in her garden or going to places where there were special birdwatching hides. Some hides were far away from roads and she struggled to walk to them, even using her crutches, so she was very glad when there were ones she could use her wheelchair to get to.

'How about a snow goose?' she said.

Lauren laughed. 'Brilliant! There are so many geese on the university lake.

Mostly Canada geese. Did I tell you that Emily was on her way to play football with some friends and she dropped the football next to some geese, and one guarded it and wouldn't let her have it back for ages? I think we should make a snow goose and put a football next to it to make her laugh.'

'We could put a university scarf around its neck!' said Maya. 'We'll make a white snow goose out of snow, not a blue one, of course.'

'A blue snow goose?' laughed Lauren. 'I've never heard of one of those!'

'It's more blueish-grey or even brown,' said Maya. 'But both white and blue snow geese have rose-red legs and feet, and pink bills. I'm not sure how we will do that.'

'Well, surely we can just have it sitting down, so that will hide the feet, and we can always make the beak out of pink paper or cardboard or something. It's not snowing now so it won't get soggy,' said Lauren, enthusiastically. 'I really like this idea, Maya! I'm glad I'm working with such a bird expert! How special that Mum left you that bird colouring book

book and pencils when she died.'

Maya smiled back at Lauren. She couldn't tell her big sister just how special the colouring book had turned out to be. Pictures magically appeared in it and when Maya coloured them, she was transported to the Magical Kingdom of Birds to help her friends, Patch, a talking magpie and Willow, a fairy princess, foil the wicked plans of Willow's uncle Astor. It had been a while since a new picture had appeared in the book, though, and Maya couldn't get back to her friends until one appeared. She checked every day, and had even looked that morning, but there had been nothing.

The two sisters made the snow goose next to the garden bench, so Maya could sit down a bit when making it, as her legs got tired when she was standing up too long. Lauren ran in to get some pink cardboard, scissors, and sellotape, and Maya took off her wet gloves and quickly made a beak, drawing in the black edges.

'I love it!' said Lauren. 'It looks like it is smiling! Emily and Pete will be so impressed by your skills! Pete's a really good artist.'

Maya suddenly felt very pleased but then a bit shy. She really wanted to do things with Lauren and Emily and Pete, but maybe Emily and Pete wouldn't want her hanging around. She shivered.

'Let's go in and get warm,' said Lauren. 'Your poor hands look frozen. We can put our gloves on the radiator and have a hot chocolate inside.'

Her phone rang. 'Oh, hi Emily! Great—so you and Pete will be here in five minutes! Maya and I will have some hot chocolate ready for you!'

Lauren gave Maya a hug. 'I'm so

proud of this snow goose.'

They took off Lauren's scarf and gently put it around the snow goose's neck. The blue, green, and white stripes of the university scarf looked great. Lauren got a football from the shed and put it on the ground as if the goose was guarding it.

'Thanks Maya—you're a star!' she laughed, passing Maya her crutches.

Maya went to her room and put her wet gloves on the radiator. She was just going to take off her coat and join Lauren in the kitchen when she heard the doorbell ring and lots of laughter. The friends were together again.

'Maybe I'll just stay in here for a minute,' she said to herself, feeling a bit shy.

She heard a tapping on the window behind her. She turned to see a black and white magpie flutter away from the glass on to the back of the big white snow goose and look up at her.

'Did that cheeky magpie fly and tap on the window?' she wondered, and felt a little flutter of excitement, thinking of Patch. The magpie cocked its head and looked at her and then seemed to be looking at the table to her left. There, she saw to her surprise, was the *Magical Kingdom of Birds* colouring book.

'That's funny—I'm sure I put it back in the bag,' she said out loud. The bag with the pencils was still hanging over the back of her chair.

The book was open, and Maya saw, to her delight, that there was a new picture waiting for her to colour in. Her friends needed her!

'I'm coming, Willow and Patch!' she said.

The new picture to colour in was of a magnificent snow goose. She took the bag and sat down, looking inside it for a black, or rose-red, or pink pencil to colour in the beak or the legs, but instead a silver pencil rolled towards her.

'That's strange—geese aren't silver,'

she said, but the pencil seemed to want

her to colour in the goose's wings silver

and kept drawing her hand to them.

'All right, magic pencil,' Maya laughed, and began to colour in the bird. Suddenly white and silver feathers, together with snowflakes, began to surround her in a whirling, glittering cloud, but she wasn't scared. She felt herself growing smaller, being lifted up into the air. Round and round she went, and then down, as the glittering cloud carried her back into the book and into the Magical Kingdom of Birds.

Chapter Two

Maya found herself sitting on a rock next to a lake. It was cold and windy, and she was glad she still had her warm coat, and hat, and scarf on. She thrust her hands into her pockets to keep warm, and was relieved to find a spare pair of gloves there. The sky was blue, with white clouds blowing around, and the landscape was very flat and rocky, with green and brown moss. On the lake, for as far as she could see, were thousands and thousands of snow geese—mainly white—although Maya noticed blue geese amongst the birds in front of her. She had never seen so many big birds of the same kind gathered together before. The noise was overwhelming. All she could hear was the hoarse honking of the geese—the air was full of the beating of wings, excited shrill barking, and high yelping cries as snow geese swam around in big crowds, or took off and flew over the lake and settled back down again. When they rose into the air and whirled around it felt like being in a very noisy snow globe, although, because of the mixture of blue and white snow geese, and the black tips on the white geese's wings, the whirling snow was a salt and peppery mixture of grey and white, rather than just one colour!

'I've heard of a gaggle of geese,' said Maya out loud, 'but this must be the biggest gaggle I've ever seen!'

'And what a racket they are making!' said a familiar voice in Maya's ear, and she turned to see the beak and bright eyes of her magpie friend, Patch. At the same time she felt two warm arms around her neck and her cheeks being tickled by Princess Willow's black curls.

'Maya! I'm so glad you're back!' said her friend excitedly, and they both beamed and hugged each other. Then they both made a face about the noise.

'Neve and Jack, the snow goose fairies, asked for our help because the snow geese are very upset and confused,' said Willow, cupping her hands and shouting above the din. 'I'm afraid it's Uncle Astor's fault again.'

'I'm sure you are not surprised!' said Patch. 'Ever since he took Princess Willow's throne and destroyed her magic cloak of feathers, there's been nothing but trouble in the Magical Kingdom of Birds.'

'What happened?' asked Maya.

'Well, normally the Silver Snow Goose appears to open the Winter Festival and then the snow geese all start migrating south for winter, but although they have been waiting here in their usual place, he hasn't arrived, and so neither will the snow.'

'If winter doesn't come, why don't they just stay here and forage as usual?' asked Maya.

'If thousands of them stay here and forage normally they will soon run out of food. One place is just not enough for them,' said Patch.

Some white and blue snow geese flew over to them and bowed. They had young geese with them.

'Welcome, Keeper of the Book!' said the dark female goose. 'We are so glad you are here. Princess Willow said she was sure you would arrive as soon as she heard of our trouble and our argument with Lord Astor.'

'What happened?' said Maya.

A white male goose shook his head sadly. 'Lord Astor heard that we have a Winter Festival and that our guest of honour is the Silver Snow Goose, and first of all he got offended that he wasn't the guest of honour and that we didn't gather to meet him.'

'Then we told him that the Silver Snow Goose had to be our guest of honour because he brought the winter and told us when to migrate, and Lord Astor said he was the one who gave orders in the Magical Kingdom of Birds, not some big silver bird,' said his wife. 'He ordered us to stay here and not listen to the Silver Snow Goose.'

'Then he flew away, very angry, and we have been waiting here ever since for the Silver Snow Goose, and for winter to come,' said the second male blue snow goose. 'Everyone is confused, and the geese are forgetting to forage, which they need to do to build up fat reserves and keep up their strength for their flight.'

At this point Maya and Willow had to put their hands over their ears because the honking was getting so loud. It reminded Maya of very loud bicycle horns.

'Is there any way we can get the geese to be a bit quieter?' shouted Patch above the din. 'Or maybe go somewhere else?'

'I'll get their attention,' said Neve, the girl snow goose fairy, who had fluttered over. Her face was as white as the snow, and she had dark eyes, short glossy black hair, and black wings tipped with silver. She wore a dress of dark feathers with red shoes and tights. She fluttered up above the excited gaggle of geese. The silver tips of her wings sparkled in the sun and caught their attention, and then she clapped her hands and brought out a silver trumpet. She blew, and the trumpet made a very loud honking noise. This was so unexpected it made

Maya want to laugh, but she could see that none of the geese were laughing— they just looked very impressed and fell silent.

'Listen, everyone,' said Neve. 'Princess Willow, Patch the magpie, and Maya, the Keeper of the Book, have come to help us, because the Silver Snow Goose has not arrived.'

'I don't believe in the Silver Snow Goose!' Maya heard one little, white-bellied, blue snow goose grumble.

'Toby!' said his smaller blue snow goose sister. 'How can you say that?'

'Well, we've never seen him—you haven't either, Tabitha, so I don't know why you think he exists!' retorted Toby.

'Well, I know we always fly south for winter when he appears in the sky above the mountain over there,' said Tabitha. 'And we always know the way to go, as he helps us along the way and appears every time we stop.'

Suddenly a new fairy flew down from the blue sky to join them. The assembled geese looked up and there was a ripple of quiet, anxious honking as they saw him appear. It was Jack, the boy snow goose fairy. His face, like his sister's, was white, with dark eyes, but his hair and wing feathers were white with black tips, his suit was made of white feathers, and his shoes were red. He looked very worried and tired, and whispered something in Willow's ear, which made her look very concerned.

Willow flew up and addressed the assembled geese.

'Dear snow geese,' she said, in her clear voice. 'Jack has told me that he flew to the mountain where the Silver Snow Goose normally appears, as a sign that winter has come and it is time to fly south, and all Jack could find were silver feathers and marks on the ground which showed signs of a struggle.'

The honking from the gaggle got louder, but Jack and Neve both signalled with their arms for the geese to stay quiet.

'See, Toby, he did come,' said Tabitha to her brother.

'I'm sorry to say, dear snow geese, that I think my wicked uncle Astor is behind this disappearance,' said Willow. 'I know he told you not to listen to the Silver Snow Goose—I think he has kidnapped him to make sure you *can't*. But do not worry. The Keeper of the Book has arrived to help us! Come, Maya and Patch, fly up here and let the snow geese see.'

'Look—Princess Willow put on my harness as soon as we heard the Silver

Snow Goose had not arrived', said Patch to Maya. 'She knew you'd be back. She has put your sticks in their quiver on my back too.' He positioned himself so that Maya could retrieve her quiver and the willow sticks the fairy princess had made for her. She used the sticks to help her get up from the rock. The ground was quite wet and boggy, and the sticks sank in a bit, but Patch crouched down low so that Maya could get on his back and they flew up to join Willow, Neve, and Jack.

There was a lot of joyful honking, and Maya could hear that some of the calls were higher-pitched than the rest, and were coming from all the younger geese.

'We will rescue the Silver Snow Goose and winter will come,' Willow said. 'Be patient and all will be well, I promise.'

The geese honked gratefully. They all had complete faith in her.

'I am so glad you are here!' Willow whispered to Maya. 'I have no idea how we are going to do this.'

Chapter
Three

Tabitha and Toby were waiting for them on the boggy ground by the lake, looking star-struck.

'I'd heard of the Keeper of the Book, but I didn't think you existed,' said Toby, shyly looking at Maya.

'What a cheek!' said Patch, pretending to be indignant. 'Do you think I fly about carrying non-existent magical humans on my back?'

Little Toby looked a bit scared of the big, magnificent black and white magpie, and Maya thought it was very sweet how his sister Tabitha came and stood in front of him protectively, even though she was slightly smaller!

'Don't worry,' said Maya, smiling down at them both from Patch's back. 'Even *I* didn't know there was a Keeper of the Book before I coloured in my first picture and came here! If I wasn't the Keeper of the Book, I don't think I would have believed in me either!'

Toby frowned a little as he worked out what Maya had said, then grinned and gave a little relieved honk and came and stood beside Tabitha.

'Can we see the book?' asked Tabitha, shyly.

'We have to look in it anyway, as I

have no idea where to find the Silver Snow Goose,' said Willow. 'I'm relying on Maya and the book to show us and help me keep my promise.'

Maya took the book out of the satchel.

'It's so beautiful!' said Tabitha. It was covered in deep-blue cloth with tiny sparkling golden figures of different types of birds all over it.

Maya opened it. There was still only one picture—the one of the snow goose she had begun to colour in silver. It was now fully silver, and glinting in the winter sunlight.

All the geese honked in awe.

'That's the Silver Snow Goose, all right,' said Patch. 'But how on earth are we going to find him?'

'That's not near here,' said Neve, frowning.

'No, I don't recognise it,' said Jack, looking at the rock the Silver Snow Goose was standing next to.

'I do,' said Toby and Tabitha's mother, a beautiful white snow goose. 'But that is way down south! That is nearly at the end of our route. We fly over that rock on our way there and back, and I always notice that it looks like a bird taking off. Lord Astor has a castle not far away.'

'But that means that Lord Astor has taken the Silver Snow Goose south ahead of us,' said Tabitha, worriedly. 'How will we know the way without having him as a guide?'

Toby's mother looked over at Toby's father, an elegant blue snow goose. 'What do you think, Andri? I feel very unsettled—I know we snow geese should not stay here and that we have to move back south, whatever Lord Astor says.'

He looked lovingly back at her. 'I

agree with you, Ana, my love. We have done the same journey every year for years. I think that I might be able to recognise landmarks and remember the way south. I will find the Silver Snow Goose, and bring him back here for the winter celebrations. The other geese seem too scared of Lord Astor to disobey him. They need the Silver Snow Goose to give them the courage to migrate.'

'I will come with you,' said Ana. 'You are my one true love, and we are never apart,' and they nuzzled each other's necks lovingly.

'We will fly with you,' said the other two couples, bravely. 'Snow geese never fly alone. We need to fly in a group to reduce the wind resistance. Andri can lead first and we will make a V-shape behind him. We can take it in turns.'

'That's still not many of us,' said Ana, worriedly. 'We would normally never travel in a group of less than 24, and mostly in flocks of thousands.'

'We can't lead thousands into a trap,' said Andri. 'And Lord Astor will see and hear us coming if there are too many of us. We need a smaller group than usual, and then we will come back for the others.'

'We will come with you too,' said Willow. 'Jack and Neve, you must stay with the young ones and all of you must insist that the snow geese eat and build up their fat reserves for the migration, and prepare for the festival.'

'But we want to come with you too,' protested Tabitha and Toby, speaking at the same time. The other young geese gave high honks in agreement.

'No,' said Willow, and Maya caught her exchanging a very serious glance with Patch. 'This is a very long and dangerous journey without the Silver Snow Goose to guide us. We don't know exactly what will happen at the end. You must stay safe and help Jack and Neve.'

'Stay, my darlings,' said Andri. 'I want

your first migration to be a happy one, and for you to see the Silver Snow Goose along the way, and see for yourselves how he helps us to carry on when we feel like giving up. We will return for you.'

Maya felt sorry for the little geese, who looked very disappointed to be left out of the adventure.

It's not very nice being left out of things, thought Maya. The little geese huddled up together, honking quietly to each other. *It's lucky they've got each other, like I've got Lauren.* For a minute she remembered Emily and Pete, and her worries about being left out, but home and everything there seemed so far away from the Magical Kingdom. She had other things to concentrate on here.

'Princess Willow,' said Neve, curtseying respectfully. 'Forgive me, but I am worried about you and Patch. This is a journey like no other. Snow geese travel many, many miles and this may take many days and nights. If Patch also carries the Keeper of the Book on his back, then I fear it will be too much.' Maya could feel Patch bristle, but the fairy was aware and curtseyed to the magpie. 'Please, do not be offended, Patch. You are a magnificent magpie, and magpies do not migrate the way that snow geese do.'

Maya could feel Patch relax. He bowed back to the fairy. 'Thank you for your kind words. But what do you suggest?'

'I can carry Maya on my back,' said Ana, 'if you can make the harness a little bigger. That way you can fly free.'

'And if Princess Willow tires, she can fly on my back at the front,' said Andri. 'Maybe even you, magpie friend,'

'I hardly think I need to be patronized,'

muttered Patch, but Maya noticed he didn't say it too loudly.

Willow and Patch must be seriously worried about this journey, thought Maya. *What if I can't help them when we reach the destination? What if this time, I'm not good enough?*

Willow found some lake grasses and wove an extension for the harness, whilst the geese who were coming with them foraged for food for the journey, walking along the side of the lake on the boggy grass and in shallow pools, expertly picking up seeds, and leaves, and roots of wild grasses and bulrushes. Maya thought it was funny how they didn't care if their heads were stained brown with earth from scrabbling in the soil. They were just really enjoying their meal and concentrating hard.

Toby and Tabitha stayed with Maya and Patch. They told them about growing up, and their nest neighbours the snowy owl chicks.

'Mum and Dad always nest near the snowy owls,' said Tabitha. 'They say it's a very safe neighbourhood when the snowy owls are there.'

They showed her their flying feathers,

and how excited they were about going
on their first migration.

'Other birds do it too, but there's LOADS and LOADS of us when we fly together, and we go REALLY far,' boasted Toby.

'Eat up then,' said Patch. 'When we come back for you there will be a long journey ahead.'

'What are you going to eat, Patch?' said Maya, worriedly. 'Actually, what are Willow and I going to eat?'

'Don't worry, Maya,' said Willow, flying over. 'I know we don't eat grass, but Neve and Jack have given us a supply of special berries to help us, and as it gets warmer as we go down south I am sure I will find more. Look, now I have a little bag, like yours, with a tent and supplies and covers for the cold nights.' Willow proudly showed off the little bag, and Maya smiled at her enthusiastic friend. *It's impossible to be too scared when Willow is about,* Maya thought. *She is always so hopeful.*

'I think we should set off without drawing attention to ourselves,' said Ana. She and Andri gave a loving farewell to little Toby and Tabitha, and the other mums and dads honked gently at their young white and blue snow geese and told them to be good for Neve and Jack.

Then they gathered together, and with a clapping of wings and quiet honking so as not to alert the others, the geese took off. They flew in a V-shape, couples beside each other, with Andri at the front, and each bird along the sides of the V flew a little higher and just beside the one in front of them.

'Andri is doing most of the work,' shouted Ana, flying next to him with Maya on her back. Willow and Patch were flying beside and slightly higher

than them. 'He is beating his wings to make upward air to lift him as he flies,' explained Ana. 'I am doing the same, but I am getting a bit of help from the upwash of air from Andri's wings, and

Patch and Princess Willow flying nearby,
and slightly higher than us, are getting
help from the upwash from mine.

'This is fun!' laughed Willow, flying
next to Patch.

'I have to admit flying is easier than usual,' laughed Patch.

'But poor Andri—that doesn't seem fair,' said Maya.

'Oh, don't worry,' replied Ana. 'We will all help—snow geese take turns to fly at the front.'

The wing beats of the geese were steady and rhythmic. Soon the overwhelmingly loud excited honking of the gaggle on the lake became more like distant dogs barking. They had begun the longest flight Maya had ever been on.

Chapter Four

Maya looked down to see a flat, mossy brown landscape with low shrubs and pools and lakes and clouds, and their silhouettes reflected in the water below as it glittered in the low winter sunlight. There were the three goose couples and Patch and Willow, but then, when Maya twisted around in her harness to look, she could see one, two, three, four, smaller silhouettes in a little V trailing behind.

Before she could say anything they flew into thick, wet cloud, and couldn't see a thing.

'Don't worry,' said Ana. 'We just keep calling to each other and working out where we are like that. We won't lose each other.'

'Are you there, Willow? Patch?' Maya called out into the mist.

'Yes,' came Willow's voice in her ear, making her jump. She felt the little fairy fly up, sit behind her, and put her arms around her. It was nice to feel her close.

'What about Patch?' called Maya.

'I'm here,' said Patch, 'flying beside you.'

'I'm here.'

'I'm here.'

'I'm here!' One by one the geese honked back, but there were four higher, rather frightened honks which were added at the end. Maya felt Ana's body tense.

'What?' she honked.

'We're here too,' came Toby's little voice, a bit apologetic and frightened.

'And me.'

'And I am.'

'Me too!' came other little honks.

All the adult geese honked worriedly.

'Keep close—can you feel the updraft?

Can you see each other?' the parents called.

'Toby—is Tabitha safe?' honked Ana.

'Yes, Mummy,' came little Tabitha's voice, sounding anxious.

Luckily, just as the anxious parental honking threatened to become deafening, the clouds cleared.

'Right, we're going down next to that pool,' announced Andri. As they came in to land they arched their wings and put their feet down, and made a few running steps before coming to rest.

'Right, Toby and Tabitha. You are in

BIG trouble,' honked a furious Ana. 'We told you to stay back and be safe with Neve and Jack. You were supposed to be helping prepare the Winter Festival.'

'There won't be a Winter Festival if you don't rescue the Silver Snow Goose,' said Toby, standing his ground.

'I thought you didn't believe in him?' said Patch, his head on one side, looking at the band of little geese. They were looking a bit scared of how cross their parents were, but defiant.

'I didn't,' admitted Toby, 'But then I saw you and the Keeper of the Book, and the silver picture in the book, and now I do. And Tabitha had a feeling we should come . . .'

Ana looked in surprise at Tabitha.

'Tabitha! You are always so well behaved! You have never disobeyed me before.'

'I'm sorry, Mummy. I just had this feeling in my tummy and in my beak and in my wings—and in my head and my heart. I just knew we should fly south with you and help rescue the Silver Snow Goose.'

'But it is such a long way,' said Andri.

'You were going to teach us all anyway—we would have come with you if the Silver Snow Goose had arrived,' said Toby. The other little geese honked in agreement.

The parental geese looked at each other.

'They're right,' said the blue female.

'There isn't time to turn back now,' said another, the big white male goose.

'The thing is,' said Ana, 'this time, because it is so urgent, we are flying faster than we normally would do, and taking less rest, so it will be harder for your young wings, not to mention that the Silver Snow Goose won't be flying with us to keep us going when it feels hard.'

'Maybe they can rest on us if they get tired,' said the big white goose. 'It's not usual, but then again, this isn't a usual situation.'

'Good idea, Charlie,' said Andri. 'Well, I can't say I am pleased about this, but we can't let you go back on your own, especially when your bodies are telling you to go south, so you'll just have to come along. I expect the best of behaviour though, from you all.'

'Yes, Andri,' honked the little geese, trying to look properly ashamed, but Maya smiled at how fast and loud and high and excited their honks were as they set off again.

The young geese were actually very

good at flying and kept up well now they were in the proper V-formation and were getting the benefit of the uplift.

Maya found Ana's warm, feathery neck very comfortable to lean against, even more comfortable than Patch, but she missed her magpie friend.

'How are you doing?' she called over to Willow and Patch, who, as the hours went by, were looking very tired.

'Princess Willow, come and ride on my back,' said Andri, and Willow gratefully fluttered over. Strong Patch bravely continued for several more hours, but eventually agreed to hover in the uplift from the wings of Charlie, the very strong white snow goose. After a while Maya glanced over and smiled to see that Patch had actually dropped down and was asleep on Charlie's back.

I've never seen a talking magpie asleep on a snow goose before, she smiled to herself. *But then again, I've never flown on a snow goose in a magical kingdom of birds before either!*

She let herself fall asleep and woke to hear the geese still honking to each other.

They were very chatty birds, always communicating and checking everyone was all right, making sure they were all together. As she listened drowsily she heard the adults telling the younger ones about amazing journeys they had taken before, and fire lights in the sky. They spoke about the Silver Snow Goose and how seeing him made them feel stronger and happier. The couples honked loving things to each other, and pointed out familiar landmarks to their children. They talked hopefully about the Winter Festival there would be when they rescued the Silver Snow Goose, and about all the preparations Neve and Jack were sure to be making.

They are so positive, Maya thought. *Miss Haynes, our teacher, would like that. She always tells us to believe in ourselves and focus on what we can do, not what we can't.*

Maya noticed the geese were very careful to take turns so that the leading goose did not get tired.

They are such lovely, kind birds, thought Maya. *They have really made us part of their flock. They work so well together as a team—that must be something we can use to defeat Lord Astor.*

They reached a forest full of pines, spruces, and larches, by the side of a large lake. Maya looked down and saw sunset touching the water of the lake below them, so that the black silhouettes of the snow geese were reflected against the pink.

'Look! How beautiful!' called Willow, who was feeling much more cheerful after her sleep, and was flying around as usual.

'What? Who? Yes, of course!' said Patch, waking up suddenly, flapping his wings and hovering above Charlie, obviously hoping nobody would mention his long nap.

'Time to settle for the night,' called Ana, and they headed down to the lake shore at the forest edge.

After filling up with shoots and leaves, most of the birds decided to sleep on the water itself at night. They floated on the water, turned their long necks and rested their necks and heads cosily along their backs, making themselves into their own feather beds. Willow excitedly unpacked the bag Neve had given her and erected a little tent for her and Maya. They persuaded Patch to come and stay in the tent instead of in the trees, and cuddled together with Patch for warmth.

They ate the special magic berries Neve and Jack had given them, washed down with clear, cold lake water in little leaf cups Willow made. They slept well for most of the night. Sometimes Maya woke and heard sleepy honks from the geese, still chatting to each other and checking everyone was together and safe.

'It's hard to keep going without hearing and seeing the Silver Snow Goose,' Maya heard Andri say to Ana.

'I know, my love,' Ana replied. 'But we have our memories, and we can imagine what he would say. I know he would be so proud of us. And we can't let him down.'

The geese were up early the next morning as the sun rose and made the lake golden, and they set off after everyone had had their breakfast. As they flew Maya loved looking across at the sunlight catching white feathers and shimmering as they moved position, or the black flickering of wing tips. Sometimes an especially tall tree or a rock, or a strong headwind, made the leading goose swerve a little, and their change of position sent a ripple down the line, like a gentle rollercoaster, as the other geese adjusted where they were.

The wind began to get stronger and the geese were buffeted about.

'Let's descend for a bit!' honked Andri, and the group headed for the ground. 'We'll forage a little and wait for the wind to change,' he said to the others. 'I think that is what the Silver Snow Goose would have said.' The other geese set off to feed.

'I hope I was right to tell us to descend,' Andri said quietly to Ana.

'You did the right thing. Well done,' said Ana lovingly to him, and they touched bills before he went to forage with the others.

'How long will it take to get past the huge forest?' Maya asked Ana.

'Days, I am afraid,' the goose said. 'It's such a long journey. The Silver Snow Goose always flies ahead of us—watching his sparkling feathers gives me energy. I only wish he were here. Just seeing him gave us courage. Andri and I are doing our best, but it is hard.'

Maya suddenly had an idea. She took the book out of the satchel. There were no new pictures, but the Silver Snow

Goose in the picture shone brightly.

'Would looking at the picture help?' she asked.

Ana looked, and honked for joy. 'Do you know, Maya, I think it would. Andri!' she called. 'Come and look at this picture with me—it will give you strength.'

Andri came over and flapped his wings in excitement, honking the others to come. They gathered round Maya, stretching out their bills and flapping their wings and calling.

'Thank you, Maya, showing us the picture has really helped,' said Ana.

'When it is our turn to fly at the front I can carry the book open at the page,' said Maya. 'And then the others can see the picture as they fly. I'm sorry you won't be able to.'

'You can talk to me about him, Maya,' said Ana. 'And I already feel so much better seeing his silver wings in the picture.'

The journey beside the huge forest was the longest flight Maya had ever been on. The geese flew steadily, encouraged when Ana and Maya were at the front, as they could look down and see the picture of the Silver Snow Goose shining in the sun. When the winds were helpful, they coasted on them, stretching out their wings and gliding, preserving their energy. When they flew down and rested a little in the middle of the day, Willow went into the forest and said hello to any little birds she found there.

As the sun set again they landed by water to roost, and prepared to spend another night at rest.

'The birds along this migratory path have noticed that winter hasn't come, and they are all unsettled,' Willow reported back to the geese. 'Some of them should have moved on, and some need to be forming big winter flocks, but they are all confused. It is clear that the arrival of the Silver Snow Goose and winter is important for everyone. The birds tell me we are still a day's flight away from Uncle Astor's castle. Ana, Andri, is there any way we can go quicker and rescue the Silver Snow Goose?'

'Yes,' said Andri. 'There are no clouds tonight, so I think, after a little break, we should fly all night too. The stars can help us. I will imagine where I saw the

Silver Snow Goose last time, and that will help me navigate. There is a light wind too, and a tingling feeling in my beak helping me. Our journey has taken long enough. Let this be the last stage.'

The other geese honked approval, and they all gathered together. Charlie and Patch had become great friends on this long journey and Patch wasn't even trying to pretend he wouldn't be hitching a lift on his back.

'We have to plan ahead,' said Willow. 'What are we going to do when we get there?'

'I think we should use your ability to work as a team,' said Maya to the geese. 'You have so much power and speed when you fly together—I'm sure we can use that to overpower Lord Astor and his guards—we just have to look out for an opportunity.'

'Let's have a look at your picture, Maya, before it gets too dark to see,' said Ana.

'Yes, hopefully it will give us strength,' agreed Andri.

Maya opened the book for them all to look at the beautiful Silver Snow Goose once more.

'Well, I feel better already,' said Ana.

Then they ran together and soared into the air, up into the clear night sky, flying by starlight over a shadowy landscape. The river below gleamed silver, and the forest at last gave way to a vast prairie stretched out below them. Maya was feeling a bit stiff and sore after days of flying, and little Tabitha had got so exhausted that she was now sitting on Ana's back. Maya was cuddling her, as they both needed cheering up.

'I am still glad I came,' said Tabitha, sadly, 'but I didn't know this journey would be so long and tiring. Mummy and Daddy and the other geese are so cheerful, but I feel too tired.'

'It's often like this when you are doing difficult things,' said Maya. 'Like when I first learnt to swim, or horse ride, or skate, or sing a solo. Sometimes I am in swimming races, and I just have to keep training even when it is hard. My dad runs marathons, and he says the hardest bit is just before the end, when you are tired but just can't see the finish yet.' *Or the darkest hour is just before the dawn. . .* and as she said that to herself, the air itself seemed to change and get warmer and, on the horizon, the sun began to rise.

'Look down there!' called Patch. 'The rock in the picture!' and the geese honked happily.

'Not long now!' called Charlie to the group, and sure enough, barely an hour later, they saw the turrets of Lord Astor's castle, flags flying in the breeze.

'All together—LAND!' called Ana, and they headed for the ground.

Chapter Five

The geese landed and waddled forwards carefully, their necks held high as they looked around for possible danger. The castle seemed deserted, with no guards, and just in front of the front door looked very pretty, with lots of green fronds laid down like a carpet.

Maya slipped off Ana's back and used

the sticks Willow had made her. It was good to feel herself walking on land again.

'It looks like Lord Astor has at least welcomed the Silver Snow Goose with respect and put down a green carpet,' said Andri, approvingly, stepping forward onto it.

Willow and Maya exchanged concerned glances as they followed behind with the young geese, who were very slow and tired, nearly falling asleep on their feet. In fact, Toby did stop and stand on one foot and fall asleep for a minute before Patch nudged him ahead.

'I'm worried about this. Lord Astor isn't normally someone who treats others with respect,' whispered Maya.

'I'm going to challenge him. Kidnapping the Silver Snow Goose is a terrible thing,' said Willow determinedly, stepping onto the path with the adult geese, with Patch beside her. Suddenly the green branches gave way and everyone on the leafy path dropped down, and a lid of branches and roots shut over them.

'Mummy! Daddy!' honked the young geese in distress as they saw their parents encaged.

'It's a trap! *Ssh!* Hide!' hissed Maya. Quickly, they managed to hide around the corner of the castle, just in time to avoid being caught by Lord Astor, who had rushed out of the front door, cackling and rubbing his hands together in triumph. He had two guards with him, who immediately kicked the green fronds aside and tied the trapdoor shut with thick vines which they wound around hooks already in the ground.

'Oh no! It was a trap!' said Tabitha, starting to cry.

I have to get the flock back together, thought Maya. *There aren't enough of us. We need the others.*

Astor peered down through slats in the trapdoor and taunted them. 'AHA! You wicked geese! I knew you would not obey me. I told you to stay in the north, but you would not listen, so it is your own fault that you are in this pit. I have your precious Silver Snow Goose. He is nothing special. I have his wings tied so he can't fly, and I ride around on him whenever I like. There is *nothing* special about HIM.'

'Wicked Uncle Astor!' came Willow's voice from the bottom of the pit. 'You have ruined the snow geese's Winter Festival and caused chaos throughout the kingdom.'

'I haven't ruined it at all!' said Lord Astor. 'It will be better than ever. Who needs winter anyway? I'm going to be the guest of honour now for those lucky, loyal snow geese who obeyed me and stayed in the north. That's better than some big silly shiny duck and lots of annoying snow.'

The geese in the pit hissed in offence.

'We like ducks, and often swim on the same lakes with them,' explained Tabitha to Maya. 'But we're not the same.'

'I know, and he knows that,' said Maya. 'I'm afraid he is just trying to upset them.'

'I've sent the rest of my guards ahead to prepare the best and biggest feast anyone has ever had,' boasted Lord Astor. 'So you can stay here and be hungry, you pathetic creatures, and you, my disloyal niece. I see you've brought your little magpie friend,' he sneered. 'He's not looking that clever now, stuck down there is he? I think I'll go and saddle up that silly silver duck now,' he went on. 'I'll go for one more ride before I lock him in a deep dungeon and get myself ready for the best Winter Festival ever seen. I might get him to pop his head over and quack "hello".' Then he strode off with his guards, looking very pleased with himself.

'What can we do?' wailed Tabitha, and all the little geese gathered round Maya, their beaks pressing into her in their panic.

'That's it!' cried Maya. 'Your beaks

can cut through the thickest of vines!'

'I know what to do!' honked little Tabitha bravely, and she ran to the trapdoor, and started pecking at the vines. Toby and the other little geese ran after her and got to work, and soon the thick, tough vine ropes had been nibbled through and Maya could hook one of her sticks through the lid and pull it open.

The pit was too long and narrow for the geese to fly out. Willow was able to flutter out, and Patch too, but the older geese were stuck.

'Toby and Tabitha, let me lean against you,' said Maya. 'Patch—can you take my sticks and put them sloping down next to each other into the pit?'

'Ah, I see what you mean, Maya!' said Patch, his clever eyes gleaming.

The magpie positioned the sticks next to each other into the pit, and one by one, encouraged and pushed by Willow and Patch, each of the geese managed to walk their way up out of the pit, using the sticks like a ladder, and rushed to their children.

'Great! We are back together. Quick—hand me my sticks, push the trapdoor back and hide around the corner, he mustn't know yet that you've escaped,' said Maya.

They watched, appalled, as Lord Astor came around the corner, riding on the back of a large goose with silver feathers, with the two guards leading him. Astor had tied a vine around the goose's body so that he couldn't flap his wings and

fly away. Everyone gasped at the Silver Snow Goose—he looked so beautiful and noble. And so sad, tied up.

'We have to work together,' said Maya. 'Willow will distract them whilst you adult geese rise up in a V and then fly down together, knock Uncle Astor off and knock over the fairy guards.'

'Yes!' said Willow. 'Then take them and fly over to the lake and drop them in. That will buy us time.'

'Children,' said Maya, 'Once that has happened you fly over to the Silver Snow Goose and nibble through the vines holding him. Agreed?'

The little geese nodded solemnly.

The adult geese took off and flew into the air above the castle.

'Hey! Uncle Astor!' called Willow, flying around the corner. 'Let the Silver Snow Goose go!'

'YOU!' sneered Lord Astor, as he saw his niece, but before he could say anything else, a furious, hissing V-formation of geese had swooped down from the sky, knocked him off the Silver Snow Goose, and tumbled the two fairy guards.

Before they could regroup Charlie

and Andri had taken one guard each, and Ana had Lord Astor, by the collars of their shirts, and they rose back up in the air holding them, their powerful wings beating.

'You can't do this, don't you know who I am?!' Lord Astor shouted furiously, waving his fists as he dangled in the air, but the geese flew off. Then there was the sound of a huge splash.

'Serve them right,' said Willow. 'Uncle can swim, but he will hate being dumped in the lake. And it gives us time to rescue the Silver Snow Goose and get away.'

The little geese had rushed to the Silver Snow Goose, but now they were next to his shining majesty they were too much in awe to say or do anything, and stood shyly, their heads bowed, looking at the ground.

'Come on kids,' said Patch. 'Get nibbling.'

Princess Willow flew up and undid the knotted vine around the Silver Goose's beak, and he gave a grateful honk.

'Thank you, my dear ones,' he said to the little geese, as they nibbled through the vines. 'I am very proud of you.

You found the strength inside to fly even though you could not see me this time. I am here to remind you to find your own way and listen to your hearts.'

'And beaks!' said Toby cheekily. 'Mine tingles when I fly south.'

The Silver Snow Goose threw back his head and honked in amusement.

'And beaks and wings and eyes—well said little goose! Every bit of you!'

The adult geese arrived back and bowed to the Silver Snow Goose as he stood, free, shining in the southern sunlight.

'You have already flown far. Now I am unbound and am strengthened by the power of the group I can bring us back by magic,' he said, and clapped his silver wings together.

There was a whirl of silver feathers in the air, and the whole group found themselves back in their northern nesting grounds with the gaggle.

'You're back!' cried Neve and Jack with relief. 'When Lord Astor's guards arrived and boasted that they had got the Silver Snow Goose and that Lord Astor would be the guest of honour we overpowered them, but we were worried.'

'We overpowered them too!' boasted Toby.

'You snow geese work so well together!' said Maya.

Ten very miserable and frightened looking guards were surrounded by hundreds of very cross geese.

'You should let them go,' said the Silver Snow Goose. 'Snow will be falling and it is too far for them to fly back. I will send them home,' and he clapped his wings and they disappeared in a glittering puff.

'That was forgiving,' said Maya to Willow.

'They aren't exactly going to have a very nice reception from my uncle!' said Willow, making a face. 'He will be blaming everyone but himself. I'm almost sorry for them.'

'Now! It is time for us to feast!' said the Silver Snow Goose to the thousands of geese, and they eagerly set to foraging properly. The sky became grey and great whirling glittering silver snowflakes began to fall, making it feel like a party.

'Ooh!' said the little snow geese excitedly. 'We haven't seen the first snow of winter before!'

'Actually, we adults have never seen snow here before either,' said Ana. 'We normally set off before it arrives.'

'Do not worry—I will be with you and keep you safe through snowstorms and sunshine,' said the Silver Snow Goose, smiling at the geese. 'But before we go—Princess Willow, here is one of my silver feathers for your cloak,' and Willow curtseyed as she took it from him.

She passed it to Maya.

'You know what this means,' said Willow sadly. 'Thank you so much again, dear friend.'

'Goodbye, Keeper of the Book,' said Ana and Andri.

'You can be in our flock any day,' said

Toby and Tabitha, rushing to lean their necks against her and wrap their wings around her, while the other little geese honked high in agreement.

'See you again, soon, I have no doubt!' said Patch.

Maya opened her book and put the silver feather inside, and as she closed the book and put it in the bag, the loud din of happy snow geese disappeared, and she found herself back in her bedroom, her gloves still wet on the radiator.

There was a knock at the door.

'May I come in?' said Lauren.

'Yes,' said Maya, carefully hanging the bag over the chair.

'Maya, the hot chocolate is ready and my friends are here. They are dying to meet you. Come and join the gang! Don't be shy!'

Maya smiled as Lauren hugged her. With Willow and Patch she had just flown on the longest journey of her life as part of a flock of amazing snow geese. They had made her welcome even though they had never met her before, and they had worked together to defeat Lord Astor and rescue the magnificent Silver Snow Goose. Why would she worry now about joining her sister Lauren and her friends? Making new friends was so much fun!

Acknowledgements

I have really enjoyed learning about Snow Geese for this story.

I would like to thank my lovely husband Graeme and our children Joanna, Michael, Laura and Christina, for all their support.

Thank you to Anne Clark, my agent.

Thank you to Liz Cross, Clare Whitston and Debbie Sims at OUP for all their editorial work on this series. I love this series very much.

Thank you Lizzie Robertson, Rosie Butcher, and Dave Shephard for making this look so lovely. Every book cover is a delight, and inside is always full of treasure!

Thank you to Hannah Penny and all the marketing and sales people at OUP, and all the bloggers and librarians and booksellers who have supported the series.

Thank you so much to Tabitha and Danielle Breachwood for your lovely enthusiasm for the series—it

makes such a difference for an author. I am so glad
that Aubrey is joining in playing 'The Magical Kingdom
of Birds' game too. I hope Tabitha likes being a little
snow goose!

Thank you as always to my friend Helen Sole, teacher,
play therapist, swimmer, cyclist, and sitting volleyball
athlete, for being my consultant on Maya's problems with
her legs.

Lastly, thanks to my dogs Timmy and Ben, who have done
absolutely nothing to help me write the book, but are great
company!

Amongst the books and online references I used to help
me write this were:

https://www.birds.cornell.edu/home/about/
https://www.allaboutbirds.org/guide/Snow_Goose/overview
https://www.nationalgeographic.com/animals/birds/s/snow-goose/

The Snow Goose by Paul Gallico (Penguin)

The Snow Geese by William Fiennes (Picador)

And a film (actually about Canada Geese) called
Fly Away Home.

About Anne

Every Christmas, Anne used to ask for a dog. She had to wait many years, but now she has two dogs, called Timmy and Ben. Timmy is a big, gentle golden retriever who loves people and food and is scared of cats. Ben is a small brown and white cavalier King Charles spaniel who is a bit like a cat because he curls up in the warmest places and bosses Timmy about. He snuffles and snorts quite a lot, and you can tell what he is feeling by the way he walks. He has a particularly pleased patter when he has stolen something he shouldn't have, which gives him away immediately. Anne lives in a village in Kent and is not afraid of spiders.

About Rosie

Rosie lives in a little town in East Yorkshire with her husband and daughter. She draws and paints by night, but by day she builds dens on the sofa, watches films about princesses, and attends tea parties. Rosie enjoys walking and having long conversations with her little girl, Penelope. They usually discuss important things like spider webs, birds, and prickly leaves.

Bird Fact File

Turn the page for information
on the real-life birds that
inspired this story.

Fun Facts

1. Snow geese can be white with black wing feathers, or white-headed with a blue-grey body and wings. These are known as blue geese.

2. All snow geese have rose-red feet and legs.

3. White and blue geese can have different-coloured babies.

4. Snow geese are vegetarians, eating grasses and grains.

5. Snow geese fly south for the winter in huge flocks.

6. There can be tens of thousands of geese in a migrating flock.

7. Snow geese spend more than half the year migrating to and from their nesting areas.

8. Pairs mate for life.

9. Snow geese may use the same nest year after year when looking after their eggs.

10. Snow geese cover their eggs with moss to keep them warm.

11. Snow geese often nest near snowy owls, probably because they help to protect them from predators.

12. Newly-hatched snow goslings are golden and fuzzy.

13. Snow goslings can swim on their own within 24 hours of hatching!

14. Families remain together through the goslings' first winter.

15. Snow geese fly in a V-formation to reduce wind drag and to stop them flying into each other.

16. Their wingspan is around 1.5m.

17. Snow geese have a dark area on the side of their beaks, known as a grin patch. It makes them look like they're smiling!

18. Geese have a row of sharp points inside their beaks, which look and act a bit like teeth. These are called tomia.

19. Snow geese are very vocal, and can often be heard from over a mile away!

Where do you find
snow geese?

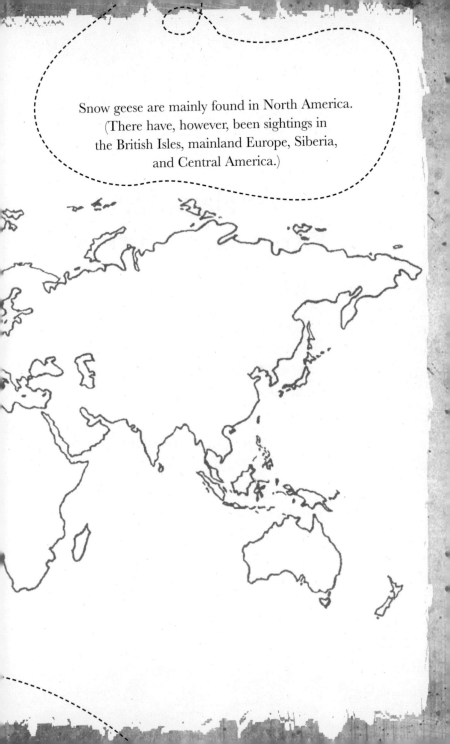

Join Maya for another adventure in
The Silent Songbirds

In a spectacular tropical glade, Maya can't believe her ears: she's attending a songbird concert in the Magical Kingdom of Birds! But all is not as it seems—Lord Astor is stealing the birds' beautiful voices to keep for himself.

Will Maya and her friends be able to return the music to the kingdom . . . ?

Chapter One

Maya and her best friend Saffron were waiting to be picked up after school. They had been at choir practice together.

'It's so amazing that they want us both to sing solos,' said Saffron. 'But you looked a bit unhappy today when they told us. Are you feeling all right?'

'I don't know,' said Maya. 'At first I

was really excited to get a solo like you, and Penny and Dad will be happy, but I just don't think I can do it. I'm not very confident about reading music. I know you have been helping me to learn what we have to sing in the choir, but it is hard. You are so used to playing the flute and singing solos at your church, but I don't do anything like that.'

'You mustn't worry. You can pick most of it up by ear, and I can always help you read the music for your solo piece too. You've got a beautiful voice, Maya,' said Saffron. 'I will sing your part, and teach you how to read when the notes go up and down. The music notes are there to help remind you, not scare you.'

'Thank you. But I still don't feel very confident singing in front of people.'

'Maya! You swim, and ride horses, and go ice skating, and you don't let problems with your legs stop you. You're the bravest person I know!' said Saffron.

'That doesn't mean I don't get scared,' said Maya, as Saffron's mum's car turned up the school drive. 'I'm just normal. I'm not brave about everything. I don't have to be brave and stand in front of everyone when I swim or skate or ride horses.'

'The thing is, you really shouldn't worry,' said Saffron. 'You are so good!'

Maya felt her tummy give a twist. 'Sorry, Saffron. Could we not talk about it any more for a bit?' she said, passing her crutches in to Saffron and getting into the car to sit next to her.

'What are you not talking about?' said Theo, Saffron's brother, who was sitting in the front next to their mum.

'Don't be nosy, Theo,' laughed his mum.

'You're as bad as Patch!' said Maya,

without thinking.

'Who is Patch?' said Theo.

'Oh just a nosy magpie I read about,' said Maya quickly.

'That's funny. Theo and I saw a magpie in your garden today,' said their mum. 'He was hopping up and down your garden path earlier almost as if he was waiting for you to come home. He obviously didn't know you were staying late for choir!'

Hearing about the magpie waiting in her garden made Maya's tummy feel completely different. Bubbles of excitement replaced the sinking feeling she had when she thought about singing. She couldn't wait to be dropped off to see if the magpie was still there, and as she waved her friends goodbye she looked around the front garden, but no cheeky black and white bird could be seen.

'Hello, Maya love,' said Penny, giving her a hug as she got in. 'How was choir?'

Maya made a bit of a face. 'I don't think I'm as good as the other soloists,' she said.

'I'm certain you are,' said Penny. 'But anyway, it's a concert, not a competition. It's not like one of your swimming competitions.'

'I still don't want people to laugh at me,' said Maya, a bit crossly.

'Why would anyone laugh at you?' said Penny. 'They wouldn't have given you a solo if you weren't good. Anyway, your dad will be home soon and dinner will be ready in half an hour. Do you want anything to drink before?'

'No, thanks. I think I'll just go and sort things out in my room for a bit,' said Maya, and she smiled at Penny.

'Fine. I'll give you a call when I need the table laying,' said Penny. 'And Maya, I got those latest swimming certificates you won framed—I hope you like where I put them.'

Maya went straight to her room. Penny had hung her swimming certificates on the wall next to the bird clock. Maya felt cheered up seeing them.

'At least I'm good at swimming,' she said. She went to her window to look in the back garden. Perhaps the magpie was there?

It wasn't.

She opened a beautiful book which was lying closed on her desk. It had a deep-blue cover decorated all over with lots of pictures of little gold birds, and the title, in gold too, said 'Magical Kingdom of Birds'. Inside were various gorgeous-coloured pictures of hummingbirds, and swans, and fairy-wrens, but after that the pages were blank.

'If only there was a picture I could colour in,' said Maya. 'Then I could get back into the Magical Kingdom and see Willow and Patch.'

This is what Maya could not explain to her best friends. Her mother had died when she was little, and had left her a magical colouring book. When a picture appeared for Maya to colour in, it meant that she was being summoned to the Magical Kingdom of Birds. There, Maya wasn't only a schoolgirl—she was known as the Keeper of the Book, and she had to help the fairy princess Willow and her friend Patch, the talking magpie, defeat Princess Willow's wicked Uncle Astor. He had taken Willow's throne and stolen and destroyed Willow's magical royal cloak, which had feathers from every bird in the kingdom, and Maya was helping Patch and Willow collect them all again. The problem was that she could only get into the kingdom when a new picture appeared, and she never knew when it would.

Maya went to sit on her bed with the

book. Suddenly she felt a tingling in her fingers as she held the book, and there, in front of her eyes, lines began to appear.

'A new picture!' she said, excitedly, and reached for the satchel hanging over the back of her chair, for the magical colouring pencils her mother had left her.

The picture revealed itself, but it was very odd. There was an open flute case with a flute inside it, lying on some blank pieces of paper. It seemed to be in the middle of a forest glade, and the surrounding trees were filled with lots of different kinds of birds. Tiny musical notes filled the edges of the page. A silver

pencil rolled out of the case as if to say

'pick me'.

'I'd better colour in the flute, then,' said Maya, and started. As soon as she had finished, the flute in the case began to flash and sparkle so brightly that she had to blink. For a moment all she could see were silver music notes around her, and all she could hear was beautiful birdsong—warbles and flutes and whistles and tweets—as she was lifted up into the silver cloud. She felt herself getting smaller and smaller and then tumbling down towards and into the book, and found herself sitting on the ground in a hot tropical forest.

More magic awaits